P9-CQE-787

In memory of Sheila Barry — editor, mentor, friend
— MF and CS

Text copyright © 2018 by Maureen Fergus
Illustrations copyright © 2018 by Carey Sookocheff
Published in Canada and the USA in 2018 by Groundwood Books

Groundwood Books / House of Anansi Press
groundwoodbooks.com

We acknowledge for their financial support of our publishing program the Canada
Council for the Arts, the Ontario Arts Council and the Government of Canada.

 Canada Council
for the Arts

Conseil des Arts
du Canada

 ONTARIO ARTS COUNCIL
CONSEIL DES ARTS DE L'ONTARIO
an Ontario government agency
un organisme du gouvernement de l'Ontario

With the participation of the Government of Canada
Avec la participation du gouvernement du Canada | Canadä

Library and Archives Canada Cataloguing in Publication
Fergus, Maureen, author
Buddy and Earl meet the neighbors / Maureen Fergus ; pictures by
Carey Sookocheff.
(A Buddy and Earl book)
Issued in print and electronic formats.
ISBN 978-1-77306-025-5 (hardcover). — ISBN 978-1-77306-026-2 (PDF).—
ISBN 978-1-77306-027-9 (FXL). — ISBN 978-1-77306-028-6 (KF8)
I. Sookocheff, Carey, illustrator II. Title. III. Title: Meet the
neighbors. IV. Series: Fergus, Maureen. Buddy and Earl.
PS8611.E735B86 2018   jC813'.6   C2017-907523-3
C2017-907524-1

FSC
www.fsc.org
MIX
Paper from
responsible sources
FSC® C012700

The illustrations were done in Acryl Gouache on watercolor paper
and assembled in Photoshop.
Design by Michael Solomon
Printed and bound in Malaysia

BUDDY
and
EARL

meet the neighbors

MAUREEN FERGUS

Pictures by

CAREY SOOKOCHEFF

GROUNDWOOD BOOKS
HOUSE OF ANANSI PRESS
TORONTO   BERKELEY

It was a warm and sunny autumn afternoon.
Buddy and Earl had just finished digging for
buried treasure and were trying to decide what
to do next.

"I think taking a nap would be nice," said Buddy.

"That *would* be nice," agreed Earl. "Unfortunately, the good citizens of this fair city expect more from us."

"They do?" said Buddy in surprise.

"Of course!" said Earl. "We're the crime-fighting superheroes Wonder Buddy and Super Earl."

"I did not know I was a superhero," said Buddy.

"You are," Earl assured him. "That's why you can leap onto the couch in a single bound and tear paper to shreds with your bare teeth."

"I had not realized those were superpowers," admitted Buddy. "What superpowers do you have, Earl?"

"I have the power of positive thinking," said Earl. "Plus, I can fly."

"I have never seen you fly," said Buddy.

"That's because I usually turn into a bat first," explained Earl.

"Oh," said Buddy. "But —"

"Excuse me," interrupted Earl. "My invisible phone is ringing."

Buddy sat quietly while Earl chatted with the mayor.

After he hung up, Earl said, "The Evil Doctor Stinker has escaped from prison."

"Oh, no," said Buddy, because this sounded bad.

"He's planning to close down the only hamburger factory in town," said Earl.

"Oh, no!" exclaimed Buddy, because this sounded *terrible*!

"To the Earl-mobile!" shouted Earl.

As fast as he could, Earl waddled over and climbed into Mom's new gardening hat. When Buddy tried to climb in after him, Earl said, "No, no. Your job is to power the Earl-mobile, remember?"

"Oh, right," said Buddy, even though he did not remember.

Seizing the Earl-mobile, Buddy dragged it
around the yard until Earl shouted, "STOP!"

Buddy stopped.

"I think we've discovered the secret lair of the Evil Doctor Stinker," whispered Earl.

"That is not a secret lair, Earl," whispered Buddy. "That is the new neighbor's yard."

"Shhh!" said Earl. "Follow me!"

Buddy nervously followed
Earl into the secret lair.
Suddenly, a deep voice
nearby said, "WOOF."

"AHHH!" shrieked Earl, curling into a prickly ball. "It's the Evil Doctor Stinker!"

"I do not think it is the Evil Doctor Stinker, Earl," said Buddy. "I think it is a bulldog."

"Tell him to back off, Buddy," said Earl in a muffled voice. "Tell him that if he makes one false move, you'll zap him with your laser-beam eyes!"

The bulldog looked so alarmed that Buddy quickly said, "Do not worry. I will not zap you with my laser-beam eyes. I do not even know how to turn them on."

"Thank goodness," said the bulldog. "My name is Mister. I'm sorry if I scared your little friend."

"I wasn't *scared*," huffed Earl as he slowly uncurled. "I was *thinking*."

"Oh," said Mister. "Snowflake likes thinking, too."
"Who is Snowflake?" asked Buddy and Earl.

"*I* am Snowflake," came a voice from high above.

An instant later, a fluffy white cat landed on the ground beside them. She inspected Earl carefully.

Then she said, "You're the funniest-looking mouse I've ever seen."

"I'm not a *mouse*!" spluttered Earl.

"He is Super Earl, the crime-fighting superhero," said Buddy loyally.

"Not now, Buddy," muttered Earl.

"He can think positively," enthused Buddy. "He can also fly!"

"Well, *I'm* more nimble than a darting butterfly," said Snowflake.

"Wow," said Buddy as he watched her twist and turn.

"Big deal," said Earl.

"I'm faster than a speeding squirrel," said Snowflake as she zipped up a tree.

"Bravo!" cried Buddy.

"So what?" yawned Earl.

"I'm even more graceful than a swooping swallow!" called Snowflake as she leaped from branch to branch.

"Can you believe what a show-off this cat is, Buddy?" crabbed Earl.

Buddy was too busy admiring Snowflake to answer.

Suddenly, Snowflake slipped.
"Oh, no," gasped Buddy.
"MEOW!" mewled Snowflake.
"Please, Super Earl — fly up there and
save her!" begged Mister.

Super Earl got Wonder Buddy to help him onto a launching pad.

Then he flapped his arms as hard as he could.

"It's no use!" he roared. "My powers are obviously being blocked by a diabolical supervillain! We're going to have to try Plan B!"

"What's Plan B?" cried Mister.

"Fetch a ladder and some cat treats," said Earl. "Lean the ladder against the tree, climb up and coax Snowflake into your paws."

For a long moment, Mister just looked at Earl.

Then he cried, "What's Plan C?"

"Buddy — tear those leaf bags to shreds with your bare teeth," ordered Earl.

Buddy tore into the leaf bags.

Snowflake slipped a little lower.

"Don't just stand there, Mister!" shouted Earl. "Help him!"

Unfortunately, as Mister rushed to help, he knocked over the launching pad with one bump of his powerful shoulder.

"AHHH!" cried Earl as he flew
through the air.

"EEEK!" cried Snowflake as she
fell from the tree.

Plop went Earl as he landed safely in the leaf pile.

Plump went Snowflake as she landed safely next to him.

"Hurrah!" cheered Mister.

"We did it!" said Buddy.

"I wasn't *scared*, you know," gasped Snowflake. "I was *thinking*."

"I know," panted Earl. "Me, too."

Buddy and Earl invited Snowflake and Mister over to play Lick the Recycling Bin sometime very soon. Then they said good-bye and headed home.

"Can we take a nap *now*, Super Earl?" asked Buddy
as he leaped onto the lawn swing in a single bound.

"The good citizens of this fair city are safe, and I'm
pooped," said Earl as he climbed up after him. "So, yes,
Wonder Buddy, we can."